BIG JIMMY'S
KUM KAU
CHINESE TAKE OUT

Written and illustrated by
Ted Lewin

HARPERCOLLINSPUBLISHERS

*To Jimmy and
everyone at Kum Kau,
and to Sam,
"Daw jea (thank you)!"*

Grateful acknowledgement to
James Cheng and Amy Cheng
for allowing us to reprint
the Kum Kau menu.

Lunch Special

(Served with Roast Pork Fried Rice)
(From 11:00 am - 3:00 pm)

L 1.	Chow Mein (Chicken or Pork)	3.20
L 2.	Chop Suey (Beef or Shrimp)	3.70
L 3.	Egg Foo Young (Chicken or Pork)	3.20
L 4.	Pepper Steak w. Onion	3.90
L 5.	Chinese Vegetable (Beef or Pork)	3.90
L 6.	Lo Mein (Pork or Chicken)	3.70
L 7.	Beef w. Pepper & Tomato	3.90
L 8.	Chicken w. Black Bean Sauce	3.90
L 9.	Curry Beef	3.90
L 10.	Broccoli w. Snow Peas	3.70
L 11.	Shrimp w. Lobster Sauce	4.70
L 12.	Bar-B-Q Spare Ribs	4.70
L 13.	Beef or Chicken Broccoli	4.50
L 14.	Sweet & Sour Chicken or Pork	4.20
L 15.	Diced Chicken w. Cashew Nuts	4.70
L 16.	Shrimp in Garlic Sauce	4.70
L 17.	Hunan Beef	4.70
L 18.	Diced Chicken in Peking Sauce	4.70
L 19.	Kung Bo Shrimp	4.70
L 20.	Buddhist Delight	4.20
L 21.	Chicken w. Garlic sauce	4.20
L 22.	Moo Goo Gai Pan	4.20
L 23.	Roast Pork Almond Ding	4.20
L 24.	Spare Rib Tip w. Garlic Sauce	3.90
L 25.	Roast Pork w. Bean Sprout	3.90
L 26.	Broccoli w. Garlic Sauce	3.70
L 27.	String Bean in Garlic Sauce	3.70
L 28.	Shrimp in Chili Sauce	4.70
L 29.	General Tso's Chicken	4.70
L 30.	Chicken & Shrimp Szechuan Style	4.70

Extras

	Pt.	Qt.
White Rice	0.60	1.20
Noodles	0.30	0.50
French Fries	1.25	2.40
Fortune Cookies or Almond Cookies		0.50
Brown Gravy	0.80	1.50

LIBRARY
OHIO DOMINICAN UNIVERSITY
1216 SUNBURY ROAD
COLUMBUS, OHIO 43219-2099

KUM KAU KITCHEN
金 球

Specializing in Chinese Food To Take Out

OHIO
DOMINICAN
UNIVERSITY™

SINCE 1911

Donated by
Floyd Dickman

S49 Seafood King

S37 Shrimp in Chili Sauce

It's Saturday at last. I wake up extra early. I'm helping out at my dad's restaurant—just for fun. Here's what the deliverymen bring to feed the customers at Kum Kau Chinese Take Out.

chicken
pork butt
spareribs
flank steak
fish
lobsters
Chinese cabbage
broccoli
green peppers
bean sprouts
shrimp
rice

I race downstairs to wait for my friend Charlie,
the deliveryman. He takes in boxes piled high with

broccoli and peppers packed in crushed ice. I carry
the bean sprouts.

The cooks have already arrived. I call each of them uncle.
Uncle Ming, Chung, Loong, Wing, Tak, Wong, Pang, and Wei
mop the kitchen floor. They scrub woks full of boiling water.
Steam rises, and the woks look like mini volcanoes.
I'm not allowed in the kitchen. It's too dangerous.

Each cook arranges his utensils—slotted spoons, strainers, and ladles. Uncle Chung sets out gigantic bowls of noodles. Uncle Ming brings out even larger pots of boiled rice. My dad, Big Jimmy, watches, hands behind his back, like a general overseeing his army of eight cooks.

At the chopping counter, my dad's cousins, Uncle Wing and Uncle Tak, prepare the meats. Chop! Chop! Chop! Dice and slice. Trim and dice. Slice and shred. Faster. Faster. Chicken, pork butt, spareribs, and flank steak—all cut up.

Chop! Chop! Chop! Uncle Wing shreds the front half of a
Chinese cabbage for Lo Mein and the back half for Chow Mein.
Chop! Chop! Chop! Uncle Loong's cleaver makes mountains of
green peppers and broccoli.

It's time to fold the menus and stack them in one neat pile. I go to my table at the front of the restaurant. The accordion shutter is still closed tight.

I wonder who I will see today.

Eleven o'clock. Time to open. Dad presses a button. The heavy
shutter goes up with a clatter. Sunlight floods through the front

windows of Kum Kau. I wait at the door to greet our first

customers of the day.

I hand a menu to Mrs. Kim, the lady from the pinky parlor next door. "Mrs. Kim! Try the Moo Shu Pork today. It's great."

"Sounds good," she says as she steps up to the counter. Mrs. Kim waves at my uncles. They wave back. She's a regular.

More customers arrive and line up in front of the counter. My Aunty Yin and my mom, Ling, wait on the other side of it, ready to relay food orders over the mike. *Ring! Ring! Ring!* Orders start pouring in over the phone.

Uncle Ming, Chung, and Wing work side by side, moving around each other like dancers in a ballet. Subgum Chow Mai Fun. Sam Gap Tai. Moo Goo Gai Pan. Buddha's Delight.

Uncle Chung mixes bean sprouts, Chinese cabbage, carrots, broccoli, scallions, mushrooms, and water chestnuts with special secret sauce. Flip. Flip. Flip. Done!

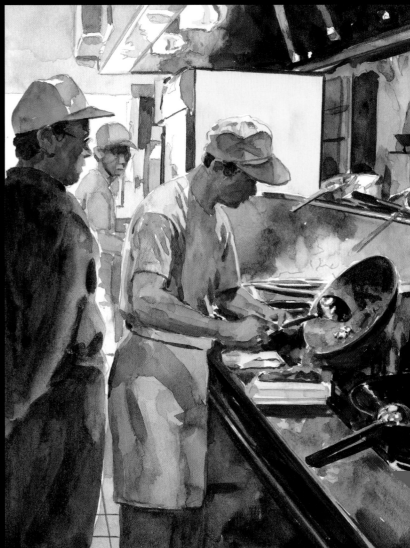

Buddha's Delight appears in less than two minutes! Uncle Chung slides the dish into a plastic container and slips it into a brown paper bag, lickety-split. He races back to his wok. Time to make Sam Gan Tai.

I'm in charge of the orders. I stuff each bag with a paper
napkin, one packet each of soy sauce, duck sauce, and hot
mustard, one plastic spoon and fork, one bag of crispy
fried noodles, and one fortune cookie. I ask each customer

"What would you like to drink? Iced tea? Soda?" Then we
add up the total. My mom and Aunty are so fast, they can
ring up the cash register and take orders over the phone at

On the other side of the kitchen, Uncle Pang prepares enormous
mounds of fried rice. Uncle Wong fries the chicken. *Hiss. Sizzle. Sizzle.*

When the lunchtime rush slows down, it's our turn to eat lunch.
Uncle Wei makes Spring Rolls specially for me. My uncles race back
to their cooking stations as soon as they finish eating. I draw pictures

Then I see the tower ladder engine from Company 119 pull up.
Tonight at the firehouse, they're having Chinese. "Four orders of
Triple Crown in Garlic Sauce and four orders of Kung Bo Shrimp!"
I know exactly what they want.

Mike the postal worker comes in for Chicken Chow Fun. Mr. Jerman always orders Egg Foo Young, and for Bob from the hardware store, it's General Tso's Shrimp. *Ring! Ring! Ring!* My Aunty Yin takes a large order for a birthday party. I start stuffing bags. Rush. Rush. Rush.

At eight o'clock the Kum Kau neon sign flashes on, glowing like a carnival ride in the pitch-dark night. I think of all the tasty dishes my

uncles have cooked all day long. It makes me hungry. I run
upstairs. It's time for my favorite dish . . .

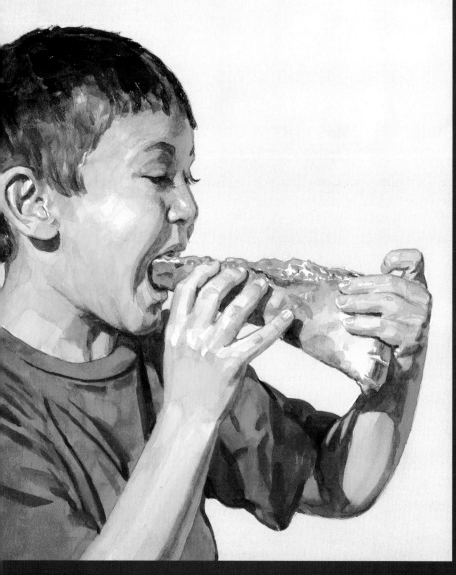

PIZ

ZA!

I like pizza but my *favorite* dish is Buddha's Delight.

A recipe for Buddha's Delight

1. Ladle a little oil into a hot wok.
2. Add bean sprouts, Chinese cabbage, carrots, broccoli, scallions, mushrooms, and water chestnuts. Flip the vegetables. Lift them out. Dump the oil. Wash the wok with boiling water.
3. Stir in special secret sauce. Let the sauce simmer and bubble until it turns into a rich brown gravy.
4. Scoop the vegetables back into the wok. Mix with special gravy. Flip. Flip. Flip. Done!

The characters in this story are fictional, but Kum Kau

is a real place in Brooklyn and a popular neighborhood

institution. *Kum kau* (金球), pronounced "gum kow,"

means "golden globe."

For this book I shot photos on location at Kum Kau

Restaurant. Using these photos as reference, I made

full-size sketches on tracing paper. Later, I added figures

that had been photographed in my studio. These

sketches were transferred onto Strathmore bristol and

carefully drawn with a 7H pencil. The finished paintings

were done in Windsor Newton watercolors with red

sable brushes.

Big Jimmy's Kum Kau Chinese Take Out
Copyright © 2002 by Ted Lewin
Printed in Hong Kong. All rights reserved.
www.harperchildrens.com

Library of Congress Cataloging-in-Publication Data Lewin, Ted. Big Jimmy's Kum Kau Chinese
take out / written and illustrated by Ted Lewin.   p.   cm. Summary: The sights, sounds, and smells
of a busy Chinese take-out restaurant are seen through the eyes of the owner's young son.
ISBN 0-688-16026-3 — ISBN 0-688-16027-1 (lib. bdg.) [1. Restaurants—Fiction. 2. Cookery,
Chinese—Fiction. 3. Grocery trade—Fiction. 4. Father and sons—Fiction.] I. Title. PZ7.L58419 Bi
2002   00-047954   [E]—dc21

Typography by Carla Weise 1 2 3 4 5 6 7 8 9 10 ❖ First Edition

108 Beef w. String Beans

Pu Pu Platter

19 Dumplings

S52 Baked Sa

137 Boneless

S55 Double Sauteed Pork

S13 Chicken w. Garlic Sauce

143 Ho

Specialties

	Plain	with French Fries	Plain Fried Rice or White Rice	with Chicken or Pork Fried Rice	with Beef or Shrimp Fried Rice
H 1. Fried 1/2 Chicken	2.80	4.20	4.20	4.70	5.25
H 2. Chicken Wings	2.25	3.85	3.85	4.35	4.90
H 3. Chicken Gizzards	2.00	3.60	3.60	4.10	4.65
H 4. Chicken Liver	2.00	3.60	3.60	4.10	4.65
H 5. Boneless Chicken	2.00	4.90	4.90	5.40	5.95
H 6. Pork Chop	2.00	4.90	4.90	5.40	5.95
H 7. Chicken Fingers	3.00	3.85	3.85	4.35	4.90
H 8. Whiting Fish (2)	3.00	4.00	4.00	4.50	5.00
H 9. American Fried Shrimps (6)	6.50	7.65	7.65	8.15	8.65
H 10. Basket Shrimps	3.75	4.65	4.65	5.40	5.95
H 11. Bar-B-Q Spare Ribs	4.95	6.10	6.10	6.85	7.15
H 12. Bar-B-Q Boneless Spare Ribs	4.95	6.10	6.10	6.85	7.15
H 13. Spare Rib Tips w. Black Bean Sauce	3.25	4.15	4.15	4.90	5.20
H 14. Bar-B-Q Spare Rib Tip	3.25	4.15	4.15	4.90	5.20
H 15. Spare Rib Tip in Garlic Sauce	3.50	4.40	4.40	5.15	5.45
H 16. Fantail Shrimps (6)	3.00	3.85	3.85	4.60	4.90
H 17. Seafood Sticks (4 pcs)	3.00	3.85	3.85	4.60	4.90
H 18. Seafood Nuggets	3.00	3.85	3.85	4.60	4.90
H 19. Beef Stew	3.50	4.40	4.40	5.15	5.45
H 20. Chicken Wings in Garlic Sauce	3.50	4.40	4.40	5.15	5.45
H 21. Buffalo Wings	3.50	4.40	4.40	5.15	5.45
H 22. Bar-B-Q Wings	3.50	4.40	4.40	5.15	5.45
H 23. Chicken Teriyaki	4.95	6.10	6.10	6.85	7.15
H 24. Beef on Stick	4.95	6.10	6.10	6.85	7.15
H 25. Chicken Nuggets	3.00	3.85	3.85	4.60	4.90

Ho

S54 Squid w. Broccoli

ster Canto